HAUNTED
HOUSES IN
MOGH'S HALF

BY

ST. JOHN D. SEYMOUR

British Library Cataloguing-in-Publication Data
A catalogue record for this book is available from the
British Library

CONTENTS

ST. JOHN D. SEYMOUR

St. John Drelincourt Seymour was born in the second half of the 19th century in Ireland. Around 1913, he came to realize that although Ireland was replete with collections of folklore and fairy-tales, the country's rich tradition of ghost stories remained largely untapped. Working with friend Harry L. Neligan, Seymour set out to correct this. The two of them put out a request for anecdotes in the newspapers of the day, and compiled the stories they received in what is now Seymour's most well-known 'non-fiction' work, *True Irish Ghost Stories* (1914). Around the same time, Seymour published his other more popular titles, *Irish Witchcraft and Demonology* and *Haunted Houses in or Near Dublin*.

HAUNTED HOUSES IN MOGH'S HALF

ST. JOHN D. SEYMOUR

THE northern half of Ireland has not proved as prolific in stories of haunted houses as the southern portion: the possible explanation of this is, not that the men of the north are less prone to hold, or talk about, such beliefs, but that, as regards the south half, we have had the good fortune to happen upon some diligent collectors of these and kindred tales, whose eagerness in collecting is only equalled by their kindness in imparting information to the compilers of this book.

On a large farm near Portarlington there once lived a Mrs. ——, a strong - minded, capable woman, who managed all her affairs for herself, giving her orders, and taking none from anybody. In due time she died, and the property passed to the next-of-kin. As soon, however, as the funeral was over, the house was nightly disturbed by strange noises: people downstairs would hear rushings about in the upper rooms, banging of doors, and the sound of heavy footsteps. The cups and saucers used to fall off the dresser, and all the pots and pans would rattle.

This went on for some time, till the people could stand it no longer, so they left the house and put in a herd and his family. The latter was driven away after he had been in the house a few weeks. This happened to several people, until at length a man named Mr. B. took the house. The noises went on as before, until some one suggested getting the priest in. Accordingly the priest came, and held a service in the late Mrs. ——'s bedroom. When this was over, the door of the room was locked. After that the noises were not heard till one evening Mr. B. came home from a fair, fortified, no doubt, with a little "Dutch courage", and declared that even if the devil were in it he would go into the locked room. In spite of all his family could say or do, he burst open the door and entered the room, but apparently saw nothing. That night pandemonium reigned in the house, the chairs were hurled about, the china was broken, and the most weird and uncanny sounds were heard. Next day the priest was sent for, the room again shut up, and nothing has happened from that day to this.

Another strange story comes from the same town. "When I was on a visit to a friend in Portarlington," writes a lady in the *Journal of the American S.P.R.*[1] "a rather unpleasant incident occurred to me. At about two o'clock in the morning I woke up suddenly, for apparently no reason whatever; however, I quite distinctly heard snoring coming from under or in the bed in which I was lying, It continued for about ten minutes, during which time I was absolutely limp with fright. The door opened, and my friend entered the bedroom, saying, 'I thought you might want me, so I came in.' Needless to say, I hailed the happy inspiration that sent her to me. I then told her what I had heard; she listened to me, and then to comfort (!) me said, 'Oh, never mind; *it is only grandfather!* He died in this room, and a snoring is heard every night at two o'clock, the hour at which he passed away.' Some time previously a German gentleman was staying with this family. They asked him in the morning how he had slept, and he replied that he was disturbed by a snoring in the room, but he supposed it was the cat."

A lady, formerly resident in Queen's Co., but who now lives near Dublin, sends the following clear and concise account of her own personal experiences in a haunted house: "Some years ago, my father, mother, sister, and myself went to live in a nice but rather small house close to the town of —— in Queen's Co. We liked the house, as it was conveniently and pleasantly situated, and we certainly never had a thought of ghosts or haunted houses, nor would my father allow any talk about such things in his presence. But we were not long settled there when we were disturbed by the opening of the parlour door every night regularly at the hour of eleven o'clock. My father and mother used to retire to their room about ten o'clock, while my sister and I used to sit up reading. We always declared that we would retire before the door opened, but we generally got so interested in our books that we would forget until we would hear the handle of the door turn, and see the door flung open. We tried in every way to account for this, but we could find no explanation, and there was no possibility of any human agent being at work.

"Some time after, light was thrown on the subject. We had visitors staying with us, and in order to make room for them, my sister was asked to sleep in the parlour. She consented without a thought of ghosts, and went to sleep quite happily; but during the night she was awakened by some one opening the door, walking across the room, and disturbing the fire-irons. She, supposing it to be the servant, called her by name, but got no answer; then the person seemed to come away from the fireplace and walk out of the room. There was a fire in the grate, but though she heard the footsteps she could see no one.

"The next thing was, that I was coming down-stairs and as I glanced towards the hall door I saw standing by it a man in a grey suit. I went to my father and told him. He asked in surprise who let him in, as the servant was out, and he himself had already locked, bolted, and chained the door an hour previously. None of us had let him in, and when my father went out to the hall the man had disappeared, and the door was as he had left it.

"Some little time after, I had a visit from a lady who knew the place well, and in the course of conversation she said:

"'This is the house poor Mr. —— used to live in.'

"'Who is Mr.—?' I asked.

"'Did you never hear of him?' she replied. 'He was a minister who used to live in this house quite alone, and was murdered in this very parlour. His landlord used to visit him sometimes, and one night he was seen coming in about eleven o'clock, and was seen again leaving about five o'clock in the morning. When Mr. —— did not come out as usual, the door was forced open, and he was found lying dead in this room by the fender, with his head battered in with the poker.'

"We left the house soon after," adds our informant.

The following weird incidents occurred, apparently in the Co. Kilkenny, to a Miss K. B. during two visits paid by her to Ireland in 1880 and 1881. The house in which she experienced the following was really an old barrack, long disused, very old-fashioned, and surrounded with a high wall: it was said that it had been built during the time of Cromwell as a stronghold for his men. The only inhabitants of this were Captain C. (a retired officer in charge of the place), Mrs. C., three daughters, and two servants. They occupied the central part of the building, the mess-room being their drawing-room. Miss K. B.'s bedroom was very lofty, and adjoined two others which were occupied by the three daughters, E., G., and L.

"The first recollection I have of anything strange," writes Miss B., "was that each night I was awakened about three o'clock by a tremendous noise, apparently in the next suite of rooms, which was empty, and it sounded as if some huge iron boxes and other heavy things were being thrown about with great force. This continued for about half an hour, when in the room underneath (the kitchen) I heard the fire being violently poked and raked for several minutes, and this was immediately followed by a most terrible and distressing cough of a man, very loud and violent. It seemed as if the exertion had brought on a paroxysm which he could not stop. In large houses in Co. Kilkenny the fires are not lighted every day, owing to the slow-burning property of the coal, and it is only necessary to rake it up every night about eleven o'clock, and in the morning it is still bright and clear. Consequently I wondered why it was necessary for Captain C. to get up in the middle of the night to stir it so violently."

A few days later Miss B. said to E. C., "I hear such strange noises every night—are there any people in the adjoining part of the building?" She turned very pale, and looking earnestly at Miss B., said, "Oh K., I am so sorry you heard. I hoped no one but myself had heard it. I could have given worlds to have spoken to you last night, but dared not move or speak." K. B. laughed at her for being so superstitious, but E. declared that the place was haunted, and told her of a number of weird things that had been seen and heard.

In the following year, 1881, Miss K. B. paid another visit to the barrack. This time there were two other visitors there—a colonel and his wife. They occupied Miss B.'s former room, while to her was allotted a huge bedroom on the top of the house, with a long corridor leading to it; opposite to this was another large room, which was occupied by the girls.

Her strange experiences commenced again. "One morning, about four o'clock, I was awakened by a very noisy martial footstep ascending the stairs, and then marching quickly up and down the corridor outside my room. Then suddenly the most violent coughing took place that I ever heard, which continued for some time, while the quick, heavy step continued its march. At last the footsteps faded away in the distance, and I then recalled to mind the same coughing after exertion last year." In the morning, at breakfast, she asked both Captain C. and the colonel had they been walking about, but both denied, and also said they had no cough. The family looked very uncomfortable, and afterwards E.

came up with tears in her eyes, and said, "Oh K., please don't say anything more about that dreadful coughing; we all hear it often, especially when anything terrible is about to happen."

Some nights later the C.'s gave a dance. When the guests had departed, Miss B. went to her bedroom. "The moon was shining so beautifully that I was able to read my Bible by its light, and had left the Bible open on the window-sill, which was a very high one, and on which I sat to read, having had to climb the washstand to reach it. I went to bed, and fell asleep, but was not long so when I was suddenly awakened by the strange feeling that some one was in the room. I opened my eyes and turned around, and saw on the window-sill in the moonlight a long, very thin, very dark figure bending over the Bible, and apparently earnestly scanning the page. As if my movement disturbed the figure, it suddenly darted up, jumped off the window-ledge on to the washstand, then to the ground, and flitted quietly across the room to the table where my jewellery was." That was the last she saw of it. She thought it was some one trying to steal her jewellery, so waited till morning, but nothing was missing. In the morning she described to one of the daughters, G., what she had seen, and the latter told her that something always happened when that appeared. Miss K. B. adds that nothing did happen. Later on she was told that a colonel had cut his throat in that very room.

Another military station, Charles Fort, near Kinsale, has long had the reputation of being haunted. An account of this was sent to the *Wide World Magazine* (January 1908), by Major H. L. Ruck Keene, D.S.O.; he states that he took it from a manuscript written by a Captain Marvell Hull about the year 1880. Further information on the subject of the haunting is to be found in Dr. Craig's *Real Pictures of Clerical Life in Ireland*.

Charles Fort was erected in 1667 by the Duke of Ormonde. It is said to be haunted by a ghost known as the "White Lady", and the traditional account of the reason for this haunting is briefly as follows: Shortly after the erection of the fort, a Colonel Warrender, a severe disciplinarian, was appointed its governor. He had a daughter, who bore the quaint Christian name of "Wilful"; she became engaged to a Sir Trevor Ashurst, and subsequently married him. On the evening of their wedding-day the bride and bridegroom were walking on the battlements, when she espied some flowers growing on the rocks beneath. She expressed a wish for them, and a sentry posted close by volunteered to climb down for them, provided Sir Trevor took his place during his absence. He assented, and took the soldier's coat and musket while he went in search of a rope. Having obtained one, he commenced his descent; but the task proving longer than he expected, Sir Trevor fell asleep. Meantime the governor visited the sentries, as was his custom, and in the course of his rounds came to where Sir Trevor was asleep. He challenged him, and on receiving no answer perceived that he was asleep, whereupon he drew a pistol and shot him through the heart. The body was brought in, and it was only then the governor realised what had happened. The bride, who appears to have gone indoors before the tragedy occurred, then learned the fate that befell her husband, and, in her distraction, rushed from the house and flung herself over the battlements. In despair at the double tragedy, her father shot himself during the night.

The above is from Dr. Craig's book already alluded to. In the *Wide World Magazine* the legend differs slightly in details. According to this the governor's name was Browne, and it was his own son, not his son-in-law, that he shot; while the incident is said to have occurred about a hundred and fifty years ago.

The "White Lady" is the ghost of the young bride. Let us see what accounts there are of her appearance. A good many years ago Fort-Major Black, who had served in the Peninsular War, gave his own personal experience to Dr. Craig. He stated that he had gone to the hall door one summer evening, and saw a lady entering the door and going up the stairs. At first he thought she was an officer's wife, but as he looked, he observed she was dressed in white, and in a very old-fashioned style. Impelled by curiosity, he hastened upstairs after her, and followed her closely into one of the rooms, but on entering it he could not find the slightest trace of any one there. On another occasion he stated that two sergeants were packing some cast stores. One of them had his little daughter with him, and the child suddenly exclaimed, "Who is that white lady who is bending over the banisters and looking down at us?" The two men looked up, but could see nothing, but the child insisted that she had seen a lady in white looking down and smiling at her.

On another occasion a staff officer, a married man, was residing in the "Governor's House". One night as the nurse lay awake—she and the children were in a room which opened into what was known as the White Lady's apartment—she suddenly saw a lady clothed in white glide to the bedside of the youngest child, and after a little place her hand upon its wrist. At this the child started in its sleep, and cried out, "Oh! take that cold hand from my wrist!" The next moment the lady disappeared.

One night, about the year 1880, Captain Marvell Hull and Lieutenant Hartland were going to the rooms occupied by the former officer. As they reached a small landing they saw distinctly in front of them a woman in a white dress. As they stood there in awestruck silence she turned and looked towards them, showing a face beautiful enough, but colourless as a corpse, and then passed on through a locked door.

But it appears that this presence did not always manifest itself in as harmless a manner. Some years ago Surgeon L. was quartered at the fort. One day he had been out snipe-shooting, and as he entered the fort the mess-bugle rang out. He hastened to his rooms to dress, but as he failed to put in an appearance at mess, one of the officers went in search of him, and found him lying senseless on the floor. When he recovered consciousness he related his experience. He said he had stooped down for the key of his door, which he had placed for safety under the mat; when in this position he felt himself violently dragged across the hall and flung down a flight of steps. With this agrees somewhat the experience of a Captain Jarves, as related by him to Captain Marvell Hull. Attracted by a strange rattling noise in his bedroom, he endeavoured to open the door of it, but found it seemingly locked. Suspecting a hoax, he called out, whereupon a gust of wind passed him, and some unseen power flung him down the stairs and laid him senseless at the bottom.

A lady, Miss Dorothy Emerson, contributes the following account of hauntings in Co. Cork:

"Three times in my life I have lived in haunted houses. I was born in the first, and we left it when I was about three years old, so I myself have no recollection of anything that took place, but I certainly saw something there, for my mother has often told me the story since. It appears that one day she was sitting in the drawing room and I was playing about. She asked me to go upstairs with a message for my nurse, so off I started, but came back in a few seconds and told her I couldn't go upstairs, as I didn't like to pass the lady in the hall. She asked what I meant, and I told her there was a lady in black sitting on a chair in the hall. Thinking that somebody must have got into the house without being noticed, she went out, taking me with her. To her astonishment there was no one there, so she asked me where I had seen the lady. I pointed to a large ottoman that stood at the foot of the stairs and said, 'The lady is there!' Mother thought it was all nonsense on my part, so she took me by the hand and started for the stairs, but pass the ottoman I would not. I took a firm stand and said, 'I won't go past the lady!' I did not make a fuss, but she could not make me go past. She herself saw absolutely nothing, but she could see that I did, so she wisely did not force me. She said nothing about the occurrence to any one, but a short time after, my nurse saw the very self-same lady in black sitting on the ottoman.

"The next house we lived in was a large country-house standing in about fifty acres of land, called 'Melton'. On the whole, this house was singularly quiet, except for one or two occurrences. When I was about five years old two cousins came to stay with us. The eldest, Elizabeth, was a girl about sixteen years old, and the youngest a little older than myself. They slept in a double-bed in the nursery, and I slept beside them on a small stretcher. Before I go any further I should say that Elizabeth was psychical, and had seen many queer things, but never up to this at "Melton". One night she woke up about two o'clock with a horrid feeling that some one was standing beside her bed. She saw nothing, but presently she felt a hand touch her. (I forgot to say that the room was lighted, as the door was kept open, and a large lamp stood outside on the landing.) The hand passed up her whole body and over her face, and she lay there absolutely frozen with terror. Just then I woke up, turned round, and sitting bolt upright, cried out, "Oh, look at the burglar, Elizabeth, he is standing beside you!" Then I started to cry, and she had to shake off her fears and get out and soothe me. The thing appeared to vanish then, because when she got back to bed nothing more happened and she fell asleep. In the morning she told herself that it was all a dream either on her part or on mine, but when my mother came into the room I informed her that there was a nasty man standing beside Elizabeth's bed in the night, and that I was sure it was a burglar, or, as I pronounced it, 'a buggler'. Fearing lest she might frighten me, Elizabeth pretended to me that I had dreamt it, but privately she told my mother what had happened. Certainly something must have been there, because she felt it and I saw it.

"Some years later, when I was about thirteen years old, I was going up to bed one night again with the two cousins before mentioned.

"The landing in front of me was in darkness, and the only light we had was a candle held by Elizabeth. I was going gaily ahead, and we were all three laughing, when suddenly out of the gloom ahead a ghastly white malevolent face appeared; it hung in the gloom exactly as if it were suspended by the hair. I was horror-stricken, and flinging my arm across my eyes to shut out the sight, I bolted back, very nearly hurling my cousin downstairs. When I looked again it was gone, but some time later when I was back in my house-residence at Alexandra College I saw the very same face hanging in the air on a dusky landing on a dark evening about six o'clock, and the appalling wickedness of its expression left me speechless.

"But to go back to 'Melton'. Twice I heard my name called, once when I was helping Janie, the housemaid, to make a bed. The rest of the family had driven off down town, and the cook was out with the fowl. Suddenly a voice called out 'Dorothy!' We both heard it, because Janie said, 'Why, there's the mistress calling, she must have forgotten something and come back!' So I cried out, 'Yes!' and ran downstairs, but there was not a soul there. Another time a cousin of mine, an English girl, and I were standing near a book-case in the breakfast-room hunting for something. We were absolutely alone in the house, as the servants were hanging out clothes, and everybody else was away. And then a voice called out, 'Adelaide! Dorothy!' and we both cried, 'Yes!' quite involuntarily before we realised that the house was empty. So we rushed out and hunted the house from attic to basement, but couldn't see a soul. Of course, we thought that the servants might be playing tricks, but we found them up in a lane a long way away from the house, and the men were in the kitchen garden.

"This ends my personal experiences at 'Melton', but two other uncanny things happened there. One night the coachman had driven my cousin, myself, and the servants to a concert some miles away, leaving in the house my father, my mother, and my eldest brother. They were peacefully reading when they were all surprised to hear some one run downstairs into the hall and laugh. Such a devilish, evil laugh! and there is nothing so loathsome as a nasty laugh. They took a lamp and, going to the hall, searched about, but could see nothing, so they went round the house, but found every place locked up and quite peaceful. The last thing that was heard there was rather peculiar. It happened to my mother. It was at night, we youngsters had gone to bed, the servants were out for the evening, and everybody else was assembled in the breakfast-room. Suddenly remembering something she had to do in the kitchen, mother started off to go downstairs. The kitchen was in the basement, and as she opened the door at the head of the stairs she was rather astonished to hear the taps in the sink being turned on and the sound of running water. Thinking the maids must have got in without being heard, she ran downstairs, to find an empty kitchen, and the taps in the sink unturned. Nor was there any sign of running water or leakage anywhere.

"Before leaving the subject of 'Melton', I must relate what happened to my nurse in the back avenue one evening while she was out chasing a runaway hen. She had an elderly friend, a woman called Dora Shine; this woman was ill, but it was hoped she would get better. My nurse, Mrs. Duke, was not thinking of her at the moment, but she looked up and who should she see walking up the lane in front of her but Dora. 'Oh, she is better, and has come to see me!' said Mrs. Duke to herself and hurried after her. Dora promptly climbed the ditch, and when Mrs. Duke got up to the spot she had vanished. She felt then that something was wrong, and the very next morning she heard that Dora had died just at the time that Mrs. Duke had seen her.

"The third house I lived in was noted for its ghosts. The

townspeople would not enter its grounds after nightfall, not even, I do believe, if you offered them money to do so. We ourselves never noticed anything in the grounds, though we knew persons who had. Many people think that a house has to be exceedingly old to be haunted, but in this case that theory certainly did not hold good. First of all, this house was built only about seventy years ago, and the builders of it died within the last twenty-six years. They had been a rich childless, couple, absolutely devoted to the house and garden, so much so that I heard that they said that they would never leave it after death. Several people declared that they had met them walking round the paths just as they used to in life. However, as I said, we never saw anything in the grounds, but the most weird things went on in the house. Besides the old couple, or rather the woman, as he was never seen, a drowned child had once been brought into the house. There was a stream in the garden which was very rapid when in flood, and this small child had been swept down, and had been taken into the house and had died there. The child must have also haunted it, as the patter of tiny feet was constantly heard.

"One Sunday evening I was sitting alone in the drawing-room with a big Irish terrier and a black cat. There had been several people in to supper, but at the moment the men were all in the smoking-room and the women upstairs. I could hear them talking faintly, but otherwise everything was very silent. By and by I heard a faint noise in the hall—which was tiled—the noise of footsteps—a child's footsteps. They made that slight pattering noise that one always associates with those flat black shoes children used to wear, which strap round the ankle. Up and down—up and down—they went ceaselessly. I listened, and suddenly I discovered that the animals were listening also, the cat in a mildly interested way, the dog with all his bristles up. He appeared terribly frightened. So I went out into the hall to see what it could be. There was nothing there, and the instant I went out the footsteps ceased. I waited for a few moments and then went back to my chair, which faced the door. The instant I sat down the noise recommenced. Up and down the tiny footsteps went, and the dog quivered and shook. So I went out again, this time hurriedly, but it was no use. Again I saw nothing. The animals meanwhile watched the door, and by the way they moved their heads I could see that they saw something. I walked in and out several times, and finally the noise ceased when the rest of the party came into the room. A short time after this one of the maids, Ellen, told me the story of the drowned child, which I had not known before. When I told her what I had heard, she told me that she, too, had often heard the footsteps.

"For the first few years we lived there I was away most

of the time at school, and as I was only at home for short intervals I never noticed anything. The first I heard of the ghosts was one day, when my cousin, Elizabeth (before mentioned), asked me whether I had ever seen anything in the room I slept in. On telling her 'No,' she told me that one night she woke up to see a woman in black standing beside the bed. Thinking that it was my mother, and that some one must be ill, she sat up and asked, 'Is there anything wrong?' Receiving no reply, she struck a match, and was very astonished to find nobody there, and the door tightly closed. This ghost was a tall woman, very stately, and dressed in stiff, black, rustling silk. On inquiry we found that the late lady of the house exactly answered to this description. My mother saw her too, or rather saw and heard her skirts. She was standing on the landing, and hearing a faint rustling she looked up to see black skirts whisking round the corner on to the next landing. One Saturday morning in the summer one of the maids, Maggie, was brushing down the stairs, and chancing to look up she saw a very tall woman, dressed in black, coming out of my room and standing near the door. Not realising for a moment that it was anything out of the common, she looked down again, and then glanced up to behold the lady moving off to the next landing, and again the black skirts whirled round the corner. So she ran downstairs to find all the womenkind out, except mother, who had not been upstairs for a couple of hours.

"This was a frightfully noisy house, especially at night-time, though a great many things happened in the day-time. Many a night I have waked up about one in the morning to hear some one run violently down the back-stairs. All night long there would be banging and rustling and noises of all descriptions, with frequent knockings on the doors. Sometimes for weeks together we would hear nothing, and then they would recommence. September, we noticed, was the worst month. There were, of course, people who pooh-poohed it all, and said the noises were caused by natural agents, rats and mice, etc. Unfortunately for this theory we had no rats, very few mice, and the cat and dog slept out, not to mention the fact that very often every one in the house got up to investigate. One night we were sure a window had fallen down, but when we went to search, they were all closed and bolted. Another night we thought every bit of china in the house was broken, as there was such a crashing from the direction of the pantries. 'Oh, goodness,' I said, sitting up in bed, 'the cat must have got in! There'll be murder in the morning!' But the morning brought no broken china nor broken anything else, and the cat was found outside as usual.

"The bathroom was over the kitchen, and the floor between was composed of single boards, therefore every word that was said in the kitchen could be heard distinctly in the bathroom. One morning I was in my bath when I distinctly heard the maids go out, one to brush out the hall, the other to do some room. They had hardly gone out when I was startled to hear the unmistakable sound of a chair drawn across the tiled floor. Scrambling into a dressing-gown I rushed out on to the landing just as the two maids, Maggie and Ellen, dashed in from the hall. Leaning over the banisters of the back-stairs I called out, 'Did either of you move a chair?' At the same moment they asked each other the same question. I ran downstairs, to find them having a consultation over a chair that was standing out in the middle of the floor, which they had left against the wall only two or three minutes before. What moved that chair? Certainly no human agency! Yet we all three heard the scraping of it, and the chair itself had left its ordinary position. The animals were upstairs with my mother, and no mouse could have done such a thing, unless it was the size of an elephant!

"One summer a Mrs. H. from Dublin came to stay with us. She was greatly interested in anything occult, but, at the same time, was not in the least afraid.

"The month was June, and the weather glorious. Mrs. H. woke up one morning to hear a great noise and rustling on the stairs, sounds which she took to be Maggie at her work and wearing a stiff apron. Thinking that it was only about eight o'clock she turned round again and went to sleep. When she woke up the second time she discovered that it was only about four o'clock, so that it must have been much earlier when she was awake before. At breakfast she related the whole story, and afterwards told it to Maggie, who astonished her by saying that she, too, had heard the noises. Indeed, she had waked Ellen up and remarked that, 'The fairies were coming for them for sure!' Footsteps had apparently gone by her door. That evening Mrs. H. was upstairs dressing for dinner; the rest of us were in the breakfast-room. By and by she came out of her room and started to descend the stairs. Somebody motioned to me to pull forward a comfortable chair, which I did. The footsteps came as far as the hall and then ceased.

" 'Why, what's she doing?' I said and looked out. There was no one there, a fact which I called out. The rest came and looked over my shoulder, and the next thing was the sight of Mrs. H. descending the stairs again, this time in person. Thinking we must have been mistaken we asked her whether she *had* been down before. She answered in the negative.

"Some time before this occurrence I was away for the week-end, and during my absence another thing happened. It was on the Sunday morning about ten-thirty. Ellen had gone to mass, and Maggie was washing up in the kitchen. The family and the animals were in the breakfast-room. Suddenly they all heard Maggie, as they thought, run violently up the back-stairs, across the landing, open the door, and bang it behind her. Remembering that she had intended to give her an order my mother started up to go and call out to her. However, something claimed her attention, and it was several minutes before she was free to go. At the foot of the stairs something prompted her to go and look into the kitchen. She did so. What was her astonishment to see Maggie there calmly washing up. Maggie, for her part, looked nearly as astonished, and her eyes grew round.

"They both exclaimed simultaneously:

"'Why, Maggie, I thought you went upstairs just now!'

"'Why, ma'am, I thought you went upstairs just now!'

"This time they did go upstairs and searched in every corner, but there wasn't a soul to be seen, and certainly no stranger could have got in without their knowing it.

"In a general way it was a very cheerful house to stay in, but now and again it seemed to acquire a gloomy atmosphere. Sometimes for months at a stretch I would sleep in my haunted room and never even think about ghosts, not even when I would be waked up in the early morning by footsteps running violently down the back-stairs. But, on the other hand, sometimes the house would be unbearable. The very air in it had an evil feeling. For a few nights I used to be stiff with terror, and I could feel that my room was full of something nasty. Once or twice people were waked up by a rap at the door, the rapper being always invited in by them, but never accepting the invitation. Several times a child was heard crying in the houses—never by the family, curiously enough, though our banshee is a crying child, but always by some visitor or stranger. One night when some one was ill the coachman slept in the house, and he asked Maggie in the morning if there was a child staying in the house, as he had heard one crying upstairs in the night. He was greatly perturbed when Maggie said, 'No.' This same Maggie had a young man, a postman, whom she subsequently married. One night he was seeing her home about nine-thirty or so. As they neared the big gates into the yard, he noticed a man leaning against them. He was going to make some remark about it, when he observed that, though apparently looking at the man, she did not seem to see him nor did she make any remark. He said nothing about it until the next day, and then he asked her whether she had seen anything. He had guessed rightly, she had not.

"Oh, it was a weird house! I have sat upstairs in my room and listened to one of the family walk upstairs slowly, rattling a bunch of keys in his pocket, and gone out to speak to him, only to find he wasn't there! Two seconds later I heard him strolling across the hall, and when I called out he assured me he had not been upstairs for some hours.

"Some people couldn't bear the house, other people loved it. My youngest brother could not stand it for more than a few days at a time. He said it depressed him horribly, and the atmosphere almost hit him in the face!"

Near a seaside town in the South of Ireland a group of small cottages was built by an old lady, in one of which she lived, while she let the others to her relatives. In process of time all the occupants died, the cottages fell into ruin, and were all pulled down (except the one in which the old lady had lived), the materials being used by a farmer to build a large house which he hoped to let to summer visitors. It was shortly afterwards taken for three years by a gentleman for his family. It should be noted that the house had very bare surroundings; there were no trees near or outhouses where people could be concealed. Soon after the family came to the house they began to hear raps all over it, on doors, windows, and walls; these raps varied in nature, sometimes being like a sledge-hammer, loud and dying away, and sometimes quick and sharp, two or three or five in succession; and all heard them. One morning about 4 A.M., the mother heard very loud knocking on the bedroom door; thinking it was the servant wanting to go to early mass, she said, "Come in," but the knocking continued till the father was awakened by it; he got up, searched the house, but could find no one. The servant's door was slightly open, and he saw that she was sound asleep. That morning a telegram came announcing the death of a beloved uncle just about the hour of the knocking. Some time previous to this the mother was in the kitchen, when a loud explosion took place beside her, startling her very much, but no cause for it could be found, nor were any traces left. This coincided with the death of an aunt, wife to the uncle who died later.

One night the mother went to her bedroom. The blind was drawn and the shutters closed, when suddenly a great crash came, as if a branch was thrown at the window, and there was a sound of broken glass. She opened the shutters with the expectation of finding the window smashed, but there was not even a crack in it. She entered the room next day at one o'clock, and the same crash took place, being heard by all in the house: she went in at 10 A.M. on another day, and the same thing happened, after which she refused to enter that room again.

Another night, after 11 P.M., the servant was washing up in the kitchen, when heavy footsteps were heard by the father and mother going up-stairs, and across a lobby to the servant's room; the father searched the house, but could find no one. After that footsteps used to be heard regularly at that hour, though no one could ever be seen walking about.

The two elder sisters slept together, and used to see flames shooting up all over the floor, though there was no smell or heat; this used to be seen two or three nights at a time, chiefly in the one room. The first time the girls saw this, one of them got up and went to her father in alarm, naturally thinking the room underneath must be on fire.

The two boys were moved to the haunted room [which one?], where they slept in one large bed with its head near the chimney-piece. The elder boy, aged about thirteen, put his watch on the mantelpiece, awoke about 2 A.M., and wishing to ascertain the time, put his hand up for his watch; he then felt a deathly cold hand laid on his. For the rest of that night the two boys were terrified by noises, apparently caused by two people rushing about the room fighting and knocking against the bed. About 6 A.M. they went to their father, almost in hysterics, from terror, and refused to sleep there again. The eldest sister, not being nervous, was then given that room; she was, however, so disturbed by these noises that she begged her father to let her leave it, but having no other room to give her, he persuaded her to stay there, and at length she got accustomed to the noise, and could sleep in spite of it. Finally the family left the house before their time was up.[1]

A lady sends an account of curious experiences in a Co. Tipperary mansion, which seem to be a blending of ordinary haunting and death-warnings.

"Twelve years ago last spring the lady who then owned this

place died, and about a week before her death a lady, who was staying in the house at the time, declared that she saw the figure of a woman in white fade into the opposite wall as she opened the door of a bedroom. We did not believe her story, and put it down to imagination.

"No death occurred in the house until last January, when an old man, who had lived here for some time, died. He had been ill here since the end of November, and died here on the 8th of January. Some time between Christmas Day and that date I went into the room where the white lady had been seen twelve years previously. It was about eleven o'clock at night, and I had no light with me. I walked towards a bed which stood in the centre of the room, when suddenly I became aware of a figure at the opposite side of it. I stood still, and stared at it. Neither of us uttered a word, but I knew from her appearance that she was not of this world.

"She was an old woman, yet not bent with years, but holding herself erect. Round her shoulders, which were plump and square, she had what appeared to be a black lace shawl. She had a thin veil over her face, so none of her features were clearly defined except her chin, which was remarkably long and pointed. Her head was covered with white curls, and a ribbon, also white, was passed round her forehead, and tied at the left side very stylishly in a bow. But the most peculiar point to be noticed was this—her head was outlined, not along the ribbon, but across the curls, by a row of faintly glimmering stars, which became smaller as they hung down at the bow. These were not arranged like a crown or tiara, but seemed as if their purpose was to light up the head. As you may perceive, I stood for some little time and took in every detail of her appearance. The room was in darkness, save for a faint light that came in from a passage through the open door behind me. But the ghostly figure was sufficiently lit up, not merely by the row of glimmering stars, but by a faint aura of light as well, which outlined all the body. When I had gazed at her for a sufficient time I thought I would go and get a candle, in the hope of seeing more clearly. I hurried away in search of one, but, of course, on my return the figure had vanished.

"Since beholding that vision some friends took me to a house some twenty-five miles away. There I happened to see an old portrait of a girl with powdered hair hanging down in curly ringlets, and a very long chin, though it represented a person many years younger than the figure I had seen. I do not know the lady of the house very well, but I managed to find out that the original of the portrait was a girl named Fitzgerald. I know that my great-grandmother had a friend of that name, a Mrs. Fitzgerald, who lived at Mitchelstown, and was styled 'The Wise Woman'. I am sure there is some connection between the portrait and the ghost, but unfortunately I am unable to trace it."

Mrs. Houlihan, now of the National Bank House, Thurles, has related to the present writer her experiences in a haunted house in Co. Kilkenny.

"When we were first married my husband was stationed in a town in Co. Kilkenny. He was then accountant in the Bank, and as no official residence was allotted to us we had to rent a private house, which we got through a local house-agent. When letting it to us the agent said nothing about rumoured hauntings, while such a thing never entered my head. In our bedroom there was a large bed, with its head against the wall, and close beside it was a door leading into a dressing-room. One night my husband was away; I went to bed and fell sound asleep, but woke up suddenly to find the figure of a woman bending over me as I lay in bed. She was dressed in black, with an old-fashioned black bonnet, but her face seemed blurred and I was unable to distinguish her features. I stared at her in that half-unconscious way that one does when between sleeping and waking, and as I did so, the figure receded towards the middle of the room and then melted away. I told this experience to my husband, but he only laughed at it, and said it was due to imagination. However, some little time afterwards, I was away, and my husband was all alone. When I returned, he said to me, 'That story of yours was not all imagination, as I supposed. I have had exactly the same experience myself!'

"My husband frequently sat up late at night reading after I had gone to bed. He told me that many times he had the greatest difficulty to keep himself from looking over his shoulder to see who was coming into the room. He never saw or heard anything, but had this indefinable impulse to look round. One night I was in bed, with the lighted candle beside me, when suddenly there came a puff! and the candle was extinguished. It was not a gust of wind that quenched it, for I distinctly heard the sound as if a human being had blown it out.

"When I was alone in that room I always had an eerie uncomfortable feeling as if something supernatural was present. I found, however, by chance, that if I altered the position of the bed I never experienced this sensation. So if I was left alone I would place the head of the bed towards another wall, and then I found that I slept without any feelings of uneasiness. But this eerie sensation was not confined to this one room; we used to put visitors into what was known as the spare room, and always, after the first night or so, they used to ask if they might have the dog to sleep with them, as there seemed to be something weird and uncanny about the room. When we were leaving the house the agent asked the maid if we had seen the ghost! I had told her nothing of our experiences, so she was able to say truthfully that we had not."

The late Mr. T. J. Westropp, to whom we were indebted for so much material, sent a tale which used to be related by a relative of his, the Rev. Thomas Westropp, concerning experiences in a house not very far from the city of Limerick. When the latter was appointed to a certain parish he had some difficulty in finding a suitable house,

but finally fixed on one which had been untenanted for many years, but had nevertheless been kept aired and in good repair, as a caretaker, who lived close by, used to come and look after it every day. The first night that the family settled there, as the clergyman was going upstairs he heard a footstep and the rustle of a dress, and as he stood aside a lady passed him, entered a door facing the stairs, and closed it after her. It was only then that he realised that her dress was very old-fashioned, and that he had not been able to enter that particular room. Next day he got assistance from a carpenter, who, with another man, forced open the door. A mat of cobwebs fell as they did so, and the floor and windows were thick with dust. The men went across the room, and as the clergyman followed them he saw a small white bird flying round the ceiling; at his exclamation the men looked back and also saw it. It swooped, flew out of the door, and they did not see it again. After that the family were alarmed by hearing noises under the floor of that room every night.

At length the clergyman had the boards taken up, and the skeleton of a child was found underneath. So old did the remains appear that the coroner did not deem it necessary to hold an inquest on them, so the rector buried them in the churchyard. Strange noises continued, as if some one were trying to force up the boards from underneath. Also a heavy ball was heard rolling down the stairs and striking against the study door. One night the two girls woke up screaming, and on the nurse running up to them, the elder said she had seen a great black dog with fiery eyes resting its paws on her bed. Her father ordered the servants to sit constantly with them in the evenings, but, notwithstanding the presence of two women in the nursery, the same thing occurred. The younger daughter was so scared that she never quite recovered. The family left the house immediately.

The same correspondent says: "An old ruined house in the hills of east Co. Clare enjoyed the reputation of being 'desperately haunted' from, at any rate, 1865 down to its dismantling. I will merely give the experiences of my own relations, as told by them to me. My mother told how one night she and my father heard creaking and grating, as if a door were being forced open. The sound came from a passage in which was a door nailed up and clamped with iron bands. A heavy footstep came down the passage, and stopped at the bedroom door for a moment; no sound was heard, and then the 'thing' came through the room to the foot of the bed. It moved round the bed, they not daring to stir. The horrible unseen visitant stopped, and they *felt* it watching them. At last it moved away, they heard it going up the passage, the door crashed, and all was silence. Lighting a candle, my father examined the room, and found the door locked; he then went along the passage, but not a sound was to be heard anywhere.

"Strange noises like footsteps, sobbing, whispering, grim laughter, and shrieks were often heard about the house. On one occasion my eldest sister and a girl cousin drove over to see the family and stayed the night. They and my two younger sisters were all crowded into a huge old-fashioned bed, and carefully drew and tucked in the curtains all round. My eldest sister awoke feeling a cold wind blowing on her face, and putting out her hand found the curtains drawn back and, as they subsequently discovered, wedged between the bed and the wall. She reached for the match-box, and was about to light the candle when a horrible mocking laugh rang out close to the bed, which awakened the other girls. Being always a plucky woman, though then badly scared, she struck a match and searched the room, but nothing was to be seen. The closed room was said to have been deserted after a murder, and its floor was supposed to be stained with blood which no human power could wash out."

Another house in Co. Clare, nearer the estuary of the
Shannon, which was formerly the residence of the D. family,
but is now pulled down, had some extraordinary tales told
about it in which facts (if we may use the word) were well
supplemented by legend. To commence with the former. A
lady writes: "My father and old Mr. D. were first cousins.
Richard D. asked my father would he come and sit up with
him one night, in order to see what might be seen. Both
were particularly sober men. The annoyances in the house
were becoming unbearable. Mrs. D.'s work-box used to
be thrown down, the table-cloth would be whisked off the
table, the fender and fire-irons would be hurled about the
room, and other similar things would happen. Mr. D. and
my father went up to one of the bedrooms, where a big fire
was made up. They searched every part of the room carefully,
but nothing uncanny was to be seen or found. They then
placed two candles and a brace of pistols on a small table
between them, and waited. Nothing happened for some
time, till all of a sudden a large black dog walked out from
under the bed. Both men fired, and the dog disappeared.
That is all! The family had to leave the house."

Now to the blending of fact with fiction, of which we have
already spoken: the intelligent reader can decide in his own
mind which is which. It was said that black magic had been
practised in this house at one time, and that in consequence

terrible and weird occurrences were quite the order of the day there. When being cooked, the hens used to scream and the mutton used to bleat in the pot. Black dogs were seen frequently. The beds used to be lifted up, and the occupants thereof used to be beaten black and blue, by invisible hands. One particularly ghoulish tale was told. It was said that a monk (!) was in love with one of the daughters of the house, who was an exceedingly fat girl. She died unmarried, and was buried in the family vault. Some time later the vault was again opened for an interment, and those who entered it found that Miss D.'s coffin had been disturbed, and the lid loosened. They then saw that all the fat around her heart had been scooped away.

Apropos of ineradicable blood on a floor, which is a not infrequent item in stories of haunted houses, it is said that a manifestation of this nature forms the haunting in a farmhouse in Co. Limerick. According to our informants, a light must be kept burning in this house all night; if by any chance it is forgotten or becomes quenched in the morning the floor is covered with blood. The story is evidently much older than the house, but no traditional explanation is given.

Two stories of haunted schools have been sent to us, both on very good authority; these establishments lie within the geographical limits of this chapter, but for obvious reasons we cannot indicate their locality more precisely, though the names of both are known to us. The first of these was told to our correspondent by the boy Brown, who was in the room, but did *not* see the ghost.

When Brown was about fifteen he was sent to —— School. His brother told him not to be frightened at anything he might see or hear, as the boys were sure to play tricks on all newcomers. He was put to sleep in a room, with another new arrival, a boy named Smith, from England. In the middle of the night Brown was roused from his sleep by Smith crying out in great alarm, and asking who was in the room. Brown, who was very angry at being waked up, told him not to be a fool—that there was no one there. The second night Smith roused him again, this time in greater alarm than the first night. He said he saw a man in cap and gown come into the room with a lamp, and then pass right through the wall. Smith got out of his bed, and fell on his knees beside Brown, beseeching him not to go to sleep. At first Brown thought it was all done to frighten him, but he then saw that Smith was in a state of abject terror. Next morning they spoke of the occurrence, and the report reached the ears of the Head Master, who sent for the two boys. Smith refused to spend another night in the room. Brown said he had seen or heard nothing, and was quite willing to sleep there if another fellow would sleep with him, but he would not care to remain there alone. The Head Master then asked for volunteers from the class of elder boys, but not one of them would sleep in the room. It had always been looked upon as "haunted", but the Master thought that by putting in new boys who had not heard the story they would sleep there all right.

Some years after, Brown revisited the place, and found that another attempt had been made to occupy the room. A new Head Master, who did not know its history, thought it a pity to have the room idle, and put a teacher, also new to the school, in possession. When this teacher came down the first morning, he asked who had come into his room during the night. He stated that a man in cap and gown, having books under his arm and a lamp in his hand, came in, sat down at a table, and began to read. He knew that he was not one of the masters, and did not recognise him as one of the boys. The room had to be abandoned. The tradition is that many years ago a master was murdered in that room by one of the students. The few boys who ever had the courage to persist in sleeping in the room said if they stayed more than two or three nights that the furniture was moved, and they heard violent noises.

The second story was sent to us by the percipient herself, and is therefore a first-hand experience. Considering that she was only a schoolgirl at the time, it must be admitted that she made a most plucky attempt to run the ghost to earth.

"A good many years ago, when I first went to school, I did not believe in ghosts, but I then had an experience which caused me to alter my opinion. I was ordered with two other girls to sleep in a small top room at the back of the house which overlooked a garden which contained ancient apple trees.

"Suddenly in the dead of night I was awakened out of my sleep by the sound of heavy footsteps, as of a man wearing big boots unlaced, pacing ceaselessly up and down a long corridor which I knew was plainly visible from the landing outside my door, as there was a large window at the farther end of it, and there was sufficient moonlight to enable one to see its full length. After listening for about twenty minutes, my curiosity was aroused, so I got up and stood on the landing. The footsteps still continued, but I could see nothing, although the sounds actually reached the foot of the flight of stairs which led from the corridor to the landing on which I was standing. Suddenly the footfall ceased, pausing at my end of the corridor, and I then considered it was high time for me to retire, which I accordingly did, carefully closing the door behind me.

"To my horror the footsteps ascended the stairs, and the bedroom door was violently dashed back against a washing-stand, beside which was a bed; the contents of the ewer were spilled over the occupant, and the steps advanced a few paces into the room in my direction. A cold perspiration broke out all over me; I cannot describe the sensation. It was not actual fear—it was more than that—I felt I had come into contact with the Unknown.

"What was about to happen? All I could do was to speak; I cried out, 'Who are you? What do you want?' Suddenly the footsteps ceased; I felt relieved, and lay awake till morning, but no further sound reached my ears. How or when my ghostly visitant disappeared I never knew; suffice it to say, my story was no nightmare, but an actual fact, of which there was found sufficient proof in the morning: the floor was still saturated with water; the door, which we always carefully closed at night, was wide open; and last, but not least, the occupant of the wet bed had heard all that had happened, but feared to speak, and lay awake till morning.

"Naturally, we related our weird experience to our schoolmates, and it was only then I learned from one of the elder girls that this ghost had manifested itself for many years in a similar fashion to the inhabitants of that room. It was supposed to be the spirit of a man who, long years before, had occupied this apartment (the house was then a private residence), and had committed suicide by hanging himself from an old apple tree opposite the window. Needless to say, the story was hushed up, and we were sharply spoken to, and warned not to mention the occurrence again.

"Some years afterwards a friend, who happened at the time to be a boarder at this very school, came to spend a week-end with me. She related an exactly similar incident which occurred a few nights previous to her visit. My experience was quite unknown to her."

The following account of strange happenings at his glebe-house has been sent by the rector of a parish in the diocese of Cashel: "Shortly after my wife and I came to live here, some ten years ago, the servants complained of hearing strange noises in the top story of the Rectory where they sleep. One girl ran away the day after she arrived, declaring that the house was haunted, and that nothing would induce her to sleep another night in it. So often had my wife to change servants on this account that at last I had to speak to the parish priest, as I suspected that the idea of 'ghosts' might have been suggested to the maids by neighbours who might have some interest in getting rid of them. I understand that my friend the parish priest spoke very forcibly from the altar on the subject of spirits, saying that the only spirits he believed ever did any harm to any one were ——, mentioning a well-known brand of the wine of the country. Whether this priestly admonition was the cause or not, for some time we heard no more tales of ghostly manifestations.

"After a while, however, my wife and I began to hear a

noise which, while in no sense alarming, has proved to be both remarkable and inexplicable. If we happen to be sitting in the dining-room after dinner, sometimes we hear what sounds like the noise of a heavy coach rumbling up to the hall door. We have both heard this noise hundreds of times between 8 P.M. and midnight. Sometimes we hear it several times the same night, and then perhaps we won't hear it again for several months. We hear it best on calm nights, and as we are nearly a quarter of a mile from the high road, it is difficult to account for, especially as the noise appears to be quite close to us—I mean not farther away than the hall door. I may mention that an Englishman was staying with us a few years ago. As we were sitting in the dining-room one night after dinner he said, 'A carriage has just driven up to the door'; but we knew it was only the 'phantom coach', for we also heard it. Only once do I remember hearing it while sitting in the drawing-room. So much for the 'sound' of the 'phantom coach', but now I must tell you what I *saw* with my own eyes as clearly as I now see the paper on which I am writing. Some years ago in the middle of the summer, on a scorching hot day, I was out cutting some hay opposite the hall door just by the tennis court. It was between twelve and one o'clock. I remember the time distinctly, as my man had gone to his dinner shortly before. The spot on which I was commanded a view of the avenue from the entrance gate for about four hundred yards. I happened to look up from my occupation—for scything is no easy work—and I saw what I took to be a somewhat high dogcart, in which two people were seated, turning in at the avenue gate. As I had my coat and waistcoat off and was not in a state to receive visitors, I got behind a newly made haycock and watched the vehicle until it came to a bend in the avenue where there is a clump of trees which obscured it from my view. As it did not, however, reappear, I concluded that the occupants had either stopped for some reason or had taken by mistake a cartway leading to the back gate into the garden. Hastily putting on my coat, I went down to the bend in the avenue, but to my surprise there was nothing to be seen.

"Returning to the Rectory, I met my housekeeper, who has been with me for nearly twenty years, and I told her what I had seen. She then told me that about a month before, while I was away from home, my man had one day gone with the trap to the station. She saw, just as I did, a trap coming up the avenue until it was lost to sight owing to the intervention of the clump of trees. As it did not come on, she went down to the bend, but there was no trap to be seen. When the man came in some half-hour after, my housekeeper asked him if he had come half-way up the avenue and turned back, but he said he had only that minute come straight from the station. My housekeeper said she did not like to tell me about it before, as she thought I 'would have laughed at her'. Whether the 'spectral gig' which I saw and the 'phantom coach' which my wife and I have often heard are one and the same I know not, but I do know that what I saw in the full blaze of the summer sun was not inspired by a dose of the spirits referred to by my friend the parish priest.

"Some time during the winter of 1912, I was in the motor-house one dark evening at about 6 P.M. I was working at the engine, and as the car was 'nose in' first, I was, of course, at the farthest point from the door. I had sent my man down to the village with a message. He was gone about ten minutes when I heard heavy footsteps enter the yard and come over to the motor-house. I 'felt' that there was some one in the house quite close to me, and I said 'Hullo, ——, what brought you back so soon?' as I knew he could not have been to the village and back. As I got no reply, I took up my electric lamp and went to the back of the motor to see who was there, but there was no one to be seen, and although I searched the yard with my lamp, I could discover no one. About a week later I heard the footsteps again under almost identical conditions, but I searched with the same futile result.

"Before I stop, I must tell you about a curious 'presentiment' which happened with regard to a man I got from the Queen's County. He arrived on a Saturday evening, and on the following Monday morning I put him to sweep the avenue. He was at his work when I went out in the motor car at about 10.30 A.M. Shortly after I left he left his wheelbarrow and tools on the avenue (just at the point where I saw the 'spectral gig' disappear), and, coming up to the Rectory, he told my housekeeper in a great state of agitation that he was quite sure that his brother, with whom he had always lived, was dead. He said he must return home at once. My housekeeper advised him to wait until I returned, but he changed his clothes and packed his box, saying he must catch the next train. Just before I returned home at twelve o'clock, a telegram came saying his brother had died suddenly that morning, and that he was to return at once. On my return I found him almost in a state of collapse. He left by the next train, and I never heard of him again."

K——Castle is a handsome blending of ancient castle and modern dwelling-house, picturesquely situated among trees, while the steep glen mentioned below runs close beside it. It has the reputation of being haunted, but, as usual, it is difficult to get information. One gentleman, to whom we wrote, stated that he never saw or heard anything worse than a bat. On the other hand, a lady who resided there a good many years ago, gives the following account of her extraordinary experiences therein:

"DEAR MR. SEYMOUR,

"I enclose some account of our experiences in K——
Castle. It would be better not to mention names, as the
people occupying it have told me they are afraid of their
servants hearing anything, and consequently giving notice.
They themselves hear voices often, but, like me, they do not
mind. When first we went there we heard people talking,
but on looking everywhere we could find no one. Then on
some nights we heard fighting in the glen beside the house.
We could hear voices raised in anger, and the clash of steel:
no person would venture there after dusk.

"One night I was sitting talking with my governess, I got
up, said good-night, and opened the door, which was on the
top of the back staircase. As I did so, I *heard* some one (a
woman) come slowly upstairs, walk past us to a window at
the end of the landing, and then with a shriek fall heavily.
As she passed it was bitterly cold, and I drew back into the
room, but did not say anything, as it might frighten the
governess. She asked me what was the matter, as I looked so
white. Without answering, I pushed her into her room, and
then searched the house, but with no results.

"Another night I was sleeping with my little girl. I awoke,
and saw a girl with long, fair hair standing at the fireplace,
one hand at her side, the other on the chimney-piece.
Thinking at first it was my little girl, I felt on the pillow to

see if she were gone, but she was fast asleep. There was no fire or light of any kind in the room.

"Some time afterwards a friend was sleeping there, and she told me that she was pushed out of bed the whole night. Two gentlemen to whom I had mentioned this came over, thinking they would find out the cause. In the morning when they came down they asked for the carriage to take them to the next train, but would not tell what they had heard or seen. Another person who came to visit her sister, who was looking after the house before we went in, slept in this room, and in the morning said she must go back that day. She also would give no information.

"On walking down the corridor, I have heard a door open, a footstep cross before me, and go into another room, *both* doors being closed at the time. An old cook I had told me that when she went into the hall in the morning, a gentleman would come down the front stairs, take a plumed hat off the stand, and vanish *through* the hall door. This she saw nearly every morning. She also said that a girl often came into her bedroom, and put her hand on her (the cook's) face; and when she would push her away she would hear a girl's voice say, 'Oh don't!' three times. I have often heard voices in the drawing-room, which decidedly sounded as if an old gentleman and a girl were talking. Noises like furniture being moved were frequently heard at night, and strangers staying with us have often asked why the servants turned out the rooms underneath them at such an unusual hour. The front-door bell sometimes rang, and I have gone down, but found no one.—Yours very sincerely,

F. T."

In one of the most southern counties of Ireland—for unfortunately we are precluded from giving any closer indication of place—there stands a castle, not hoary with age, but a modern antique, though as stoutly and strongly built as if it dated from the days of yore, which is said to have been erected by an eccentric member of a titled family. This castle is surrounded by a spacious walled-in courtyard, to which admission is obtained through a large gateway. The entrance-door of this castle is approached by two or three steps. On entering, the visitor finds that a flight of steps on his left leads down to a basement or cellar. A short straight flight of stone steps on his right conducts him to the hall; while the upper stories are reached by a stone staircase, not spiral, as is usually the case, but straight, though the flights go in a somewhat zigzag manner.

This place is haunted by a peculiar noise, which is heard periodically. A gentleman, whom the present writer has known intimately from childhood, relates his experience of this noise as follows:

"My regiment went out for training every summer to this

castle, and our tents were pitched inside the courtyard. One night two or three other officers and myself were standing in the courtyard chatting before retiring to our respective tents. We were only a few yards from the entrance-door of the castle, and our thoughts were on anything save ghosts. The night was perfectly still. Suddenly we heard within the castle a most appalling uproar. It sounded exactly as if some one had filled a clothes-basket with crockery and then flung the contents headlong down the stone stairs. Crash! Crash! Crash! The imaginary china seemed to be rattling and leaping from step to step until it reached the hall, or thereabouts, when it ceased as suddenly as it had begun. On the moment we determined to investigate the matter. We rushed to the entrance door, but finding this locked, managed to make our way in through a window. We then closely examined the entire building from top to bottom, but found nothing out of place or damaged. Some of the rooms were used as offices by us, and the furniture was not stirred. There was even some china belonging to the regiment stored there, and this we found absolutely intact. So we made our way out again, no nearer the solution of the mystery than when we entered.

"I have heard the noise myself, and so have others, on different occasions during our periods of training. It always seemed as if it commenced at the very top of the building, which was four stories high (not counting the basement), as well as I remember, and continued until it reached the hall or thereabouts; it never appeared to go down into the cellar. Sometimes the noise lasted as long as it would take an imaginary basket full of china to fall the distance I have mentioned; at other times it seemed to last somewhat longer. It was always heard at night, never in the daytime, so far as I am aware. We got quite used to it in time, and when we heard it used to say, 'Oh, there's the ghost at it again!' "

"Kilman" Castle, in the heart of Ireland—the name is obviously a pseudonym—has been described as perhaps the worst haunted mansion in the British Isles. That it deserves this doubtful recommendation, we cannot say; but at all events the ordinary reader will be prepared to admit that it contains sufficient "ghosts" to satisfy the most greedy ghost - hunter. Some years ago the present writer paid a visit to this castle, and was shown all over it one morning by the mistress of the house, who, under the *nom de plume* of "Andrew Merry", has published novels dealing with Irish life, and has also contributed articles on the ghostly phenomena of her house to the *Occult Review* (December 1908 and January 1909).

The place itself is a grim, grey, bare building. The central portion, in which is the entrance-hall, is a square castle of the usual type; it is built on a rock, and a slight batter from base to summit gives an added appearance of strength and solidity. On either side of the castle are more modern wings, one of which terminates in what is known as the "Priest's House".[1]

Now to the ghosts. The top story of the central tower is a large, well-lighted apartment, called the "Chapel", having evidently served that purpose in times past. At one end is what is said to be an *oubliette*, now almost filled up. Occasionally in the evenings, people walking along the roads or in the fields see the windows of this chapel lighted up for a few seconds as if many lamps were suddenly brought into it. This is certainly *not* due to servants; from our experience we can testify that it is the last place on earth that a domestic would enter after dark. It is also said that a treasure is buried somewhere in or around the castle. The legend runs that an ancestor was about to be taken to Dublin on a charge of rebellion, and, fearing he would never return, made the best of the time left to him by burying somewhere a crock full of gold and jewels. Contrary to expectation, he *did* return; but his long confinement had turned his brain, and he could never remember the spot where he had deposited his treasure years before. Some time ago a lady, a Miss B., who was decidedly psychic, was invited to Kilman Castle in the hope that she would be able to locate the whereabouts of this treasure. In this respect she failed, unfortunately, but gave, nevertheless, a curious example of her power. As she walked through the hall with her hostess, she suddenly laid her hand upon the bare stone wall, and remarked, "There is something uncanny here, but I don't know what it is." In that very spot, some time previously, two skeletons had been discovered walled up.

The sequel to this is curious. Some time after, Miss B. was either trying automatic writing, or else was at a séance (we forget which), when a message came to her from the Unseen, stating that the treasure at Kilman Castle was concealed in the chapel under the tessellated pavement near the altar. But this spirit was either a "lying spirit", or else a most impish one, for there is no trace of an altar, and it is impossible to say, from the style of the room, where it stood; while the tessellated pavement (if it exists) is so covered with the debris of the former roof that it would be almost impossible to have it thoroughly cleared.

There is as well a miscellaneous assortment of ghosts. A monk with tonsure and cowl walks in at one window of the Priest's House, and out at another. There is also a little old man, dressed in the antique garb of a green cut-away coat, knee breeches, and buckled shoes: he is sometimes accompanied by an old lady in similar old-fashioned costume. Another ghost has a penchant for lying on the bed beside its lawful and earthly occupant; nothing is seen, but a great weight is felt, and a consequent deep impression made on the bedclothes.

The lady of the house states that she has a number of letters from friends, in which they relate the supernatural experiences they had while staying at the castle. In one of these the writer, a gentleman, was awakened one night by an extraordinary feeling of intense cold at his heart. He then saw in front of him a tall female figure, clothed from head to foot in red, and with its right hand raised menacingly in the air: the light which illuminated the figure was from within. He lit a match, and sprang out of bed, but the room was empty. He went back to bed, and saw nothing more that night, except that several times the same cold feeling gripped his heart, though to the touch the flesh was quite warm.

But of all the ghosts in that well-haunted house the most unpleasant is that inexplicable thing that is usually called "It". The lady of the house described to the present writer her personal experience of this phantom. High up round one side of the hall runs a gallery which connects with some of the bedrooms. One evening she was in this gallery leaning on the balustrade, and looking down into the hall. Suddenly she felt two hands laid on her shoulders; she turned round sharply, and saw "It" standing close beside her. She described it as being human in shape, and about four feet high; the eyes were like two black holes in the face, and the whole figure seemed as if it were made of grey cotton-wool, while it was accompanied by a most appalling stench, such as would come from a decaying human body. The lady got a shock, from which she did not recover for a long time.

An even more unpleasant account of a haunting was told to Mr. Reginald B. Span by the Rev. F. Bennet, of the Anglican Church, Arizona, U.S.A. Some friends of the latter's rented an old castle in the South of Ireland—a very ancient and picturesque building standing in beautiful and extensive grounds. They heard some rumours of the place being haunted, but as they were getting it at a low rent this did not concern them.

The new tenants, the A. family, were delighted with their residence, and for some time nothing uncanny was noticed. After a little, however, the servants complained of footsteps outside their doors and of some one attempting to enter their rooms, but this was put down to imagination induced by the tales told to them by the village people. One night Mrs. A. was late in retiring—her husband had gone to Dublin—and was sitting by her bedroom fire. Perfect stillness reigned through the house. Suddenly the silence was broken by the sharp bang of a door in the corridor where the room was, followed by the sound of footsteps—but most peculiar footsteps—moving in a stealthy way down the corridor. She opened the door, and went outside with a lighted candle to see who or what it was. At the end of the passage she saw in the dim light an extraordinary-looking figure moving with a clumsy, shambling, but stealthy tread towards the staircase. She held the light above her head to get a better view, and the creature turned round for an instant and looked at her, disclosing a human face of revolting hideousness surmounting what appeared to be the body of a huge ape—and then in an instant it vanished.

Shrieking with terror she rushed back to her room. One of her daughters came hurriedly in at the outcry, and on learning what had been seen, tried to persuade her mother that it was nothing but a nightmare. The next day Mr. A. returned, and his wife decided to say nothing to him about her experience.

A few nights later Mr. A. was coming up the stairs from the big entrance-hall, where he had been smoking and reading before retiring, when he heard a weird, blood-curdling sort of laugh, and looking up to the landing above saw a tall ungainly figure leaning over the banisters looking down at him. He saw its face distinctly, which was that of a man of about forty years of age—deathly white and hairless—with the most horribly malignant expression. At the moment the features were distorted by a hideous grin, and the form shook with laughter, while the eyes seemed to gleam like red-hot coals. The hands and arms resting on the rail of the banister were like those of an ape, while the whole form was covered with thick reddish-brown hair. Mr. A. rushed up the stairs towards it, whereupon it gave peal after peal of fiendish laughter, and then vanished.

Mrs. A. and her son and daughter heard the noise of laughing, and they joined Mr. A., who recounted his experience, whereupon Mrs. A. told what had befallen her a few nights previously. They thereupon determined to search all the rooms, which they did thoroughly without finding a trace of anything. As the servants occupied another part of the house they had heard nothing, and of course were kept in ignorance. They decided that they would not relinquish their tenancy, but determined to keep a sharp look-out and try and get at the bottom of the mystery. Nothing further happened for some time. There were occasionally queer noises heard in the early hours of morning, such as footsteps, muffled cries and groans, and banging of doors, none of which they could account for, but which did not disturb them much.

However, a climax came which caused them to leave. Miss A. was one afternoon in the drawing-room arranging some flowers. She was standing at one of the tables when she heard a noise behind her, and felt two hands laid on her shoulders. Thinking it was a girl friend who was then in the house she exclaimed lightly, "Oh, there you are!" and on turning round to greet her, came face to face with a most loathsome-looking creature which had just removed its hands from her shoulders and was chuckling with diabolical glee. It was neither human being nor animal—and instead of clothing was covered with hair like an orang-outang: it stood over six feet high and had a most repulsive appearance. It was, in fact, the creature which had been seen twice before, at night-time. Feeling sick and faint with horror and disgust she gave a piercing shriek, and just as her friend entered the room the apparition disappeared, and Miss A. fell back in a dead faint. The girl who came in so opportunely just caught a glimpse of the ghost before it vanished. After this episide the A.'s thought it would be advisable to go, and accordingly left T——Castle as soon as they conveniently could.

[1] For September 1913.

[1] *Journal of American S.P.R.* for September 1913.

[1] The castle has since been burnt.